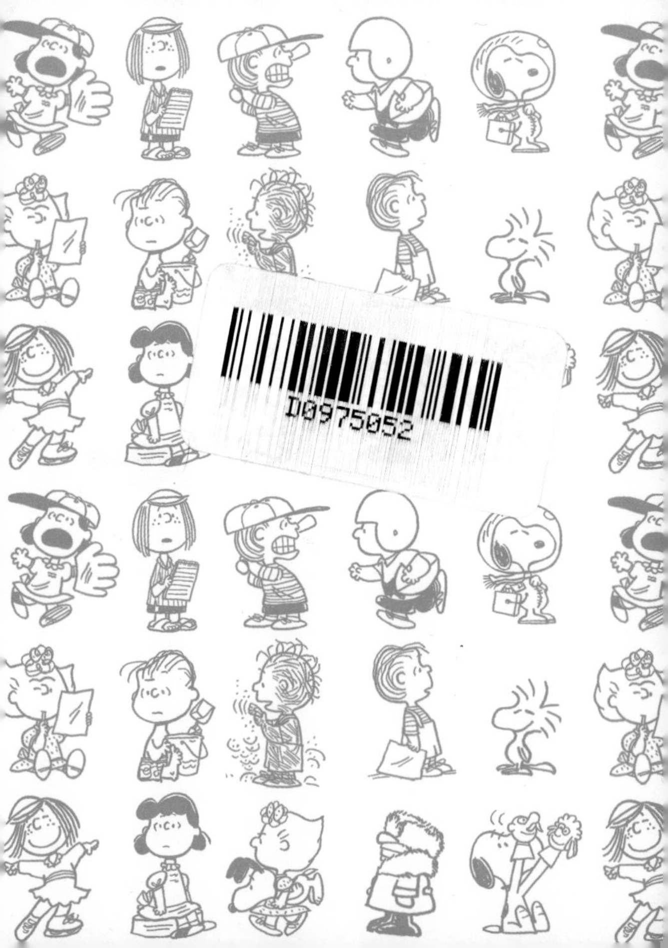

Be
Brave

PEANUTS WISDOM TO CARRY YOU THROUGH

Copyright © 2013 by Peanuts Worldwide LLC
Published by Running Press,
A Member of the Perseus Books Group
All rights reserved under the Pan-American and International
Copyright Conventions

Printed in China

Books published by Running Press are available at special discounts for bulk purchases in the United States by corporations, institutions, and other organizations. For more information, please contact the Special Markets Department at the Perseus Books Group, 2300 Chestnut Street, Suite 200, Philadelphia, PA 19103, or call (800) 810-4145, ext. 5000, or e-mail special.markets@perseusbooks.com.

ISBN 978-0-7624-4861-6
Library of Congress Control Number: 2012954475

9   8   7   6   5   4   3
Digit on the right indicates the number of this printing

Artwork created by Charles M. Schulz
For Charles M. Schulz Creative Associates: pencils by Vicki Scott,
inks by Paige Braddock, colors by Alexis E. Fajardo
Designed by Rob Williams
Edited by Marlo Scrimizzi
Typography: Archer, Bemio, BigCaslon, Carton, Chowderhead, Clarendon,
Din, Futura, Gill Sans, Hypatia Sans, Mission Script and Neutra

Running Press Book Publishers
2300 Chestnut Street
Philadelphia, PA 19103-4371

Visit us on the web!
www.runningpress.com
www.snoopy.com

Be
Brave

PEANUTS WISDOM TO CARRY YOU THROUGH

Based on the comic strip, PEANUTS,
by Charles M. Schulz

Running Press
PHILADELPHIA · LONDON

"If you grit your teeth
and show real determination,
you'll always have a chance."

—*Charles M. Schulz*

Be
FIERCE

"Only the bravest and most dedicated pilot would fly in weather like this."
    —*Snoopy*

Be
PERSISTENT

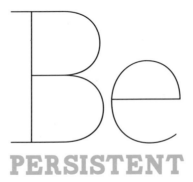

"I'm well worth all the time it takes to understand me. In other words, to know me is to love me!"
—*Lucy*

Be
Ambitious

Be
UNSTOPPABLE

Be
RESOURCEFUL

Be
Adventurous

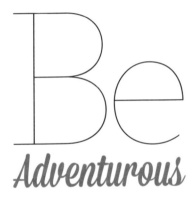

Be
UNIQUE

Be
Creative

Be
HEALTHY

Peppermint Patty: I've decided to start eating more vegetables for lunch.
Marcie: Carrot cake is not a vegetable. . . .

Be
CONFIDENT

"If I wink at that little red-haired girl, maybe she'll notice me."
   —*Charlie Brown*

Be

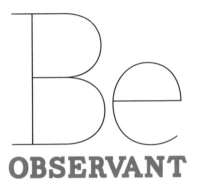

OBSERVANT

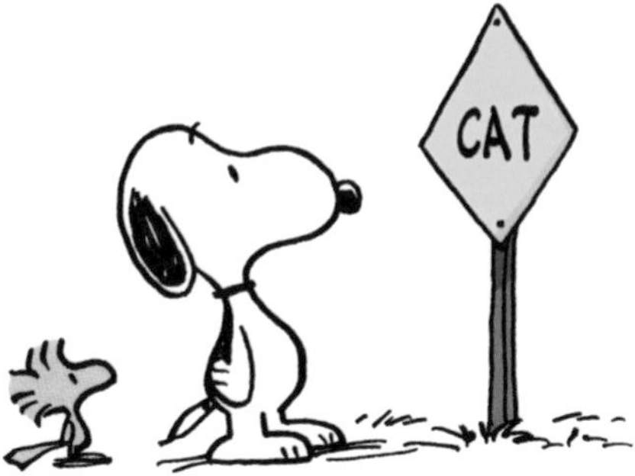
CAT

Be
A Leader

"Here's the world famous sergeant-major of the foreign legion leading his troops on a mission. As they leave civilization, they approach the desert with its miles and miles of burning sand. . . ."
—*Snoopy*

Be
REASONABLE

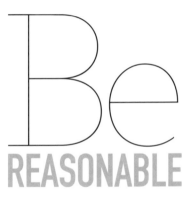

"Never worry about tomorrow, Charlie Brown. Tomorrow will soon be today, and before you know it, today will be yesterday."
   —*Lucy*

Be
BRILLIANT

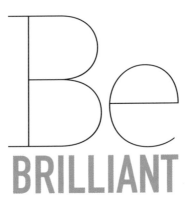

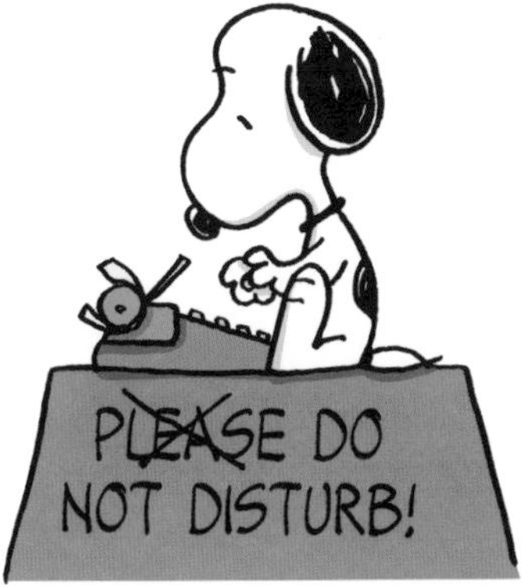
PLEASE DO
NOT DISTURB!

Be ASSERTIVE

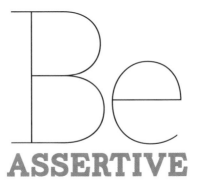

"I introduced myself to our principal. It's a good thing I did. He had never heard of me. Tomorrow I'm gonna check out all the emergency exits, then I'm gonna introduce myself to the nurse and custodian."
　　—Rerun

Be
ACTIVE

FORE!

Marcie: If I'm going to be your caddy, sir, I thought I should learn some golf expressions. "Drive for show . . . Putt for dough."

Peppermint Patty: That was good, Marcie. What other ones did you learn?

Be
Clever

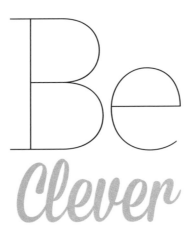

"My grampa says life is full of hills. Some days it's uphill . . . Some days it's downhill. Lately, he says, it's been mostly side hill."
    —Franklin

Be

INDEPENDENT

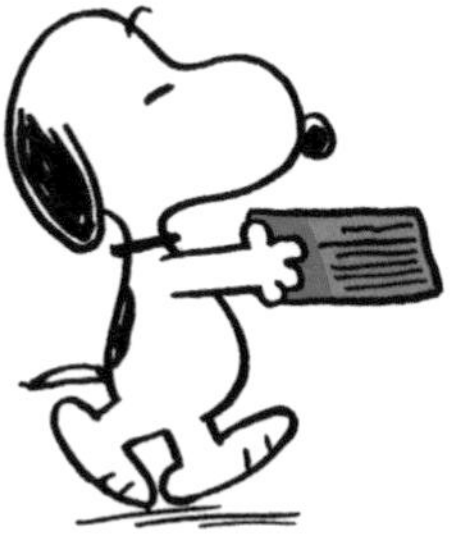

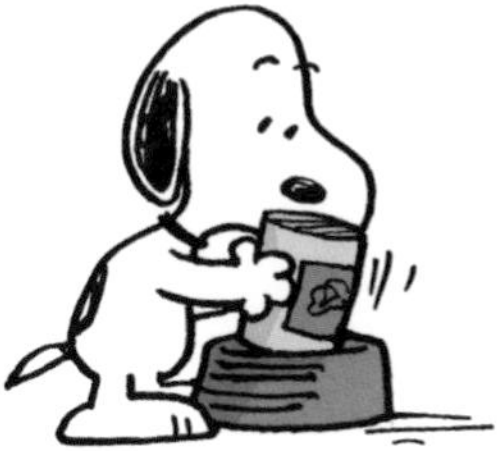

Be
SMART

"I've been reading a history of the world. I never realized so many people have lived on the earth. I feel sorry for them. What fun was it without having me around?"
    —*Sally*

Be
HONEST

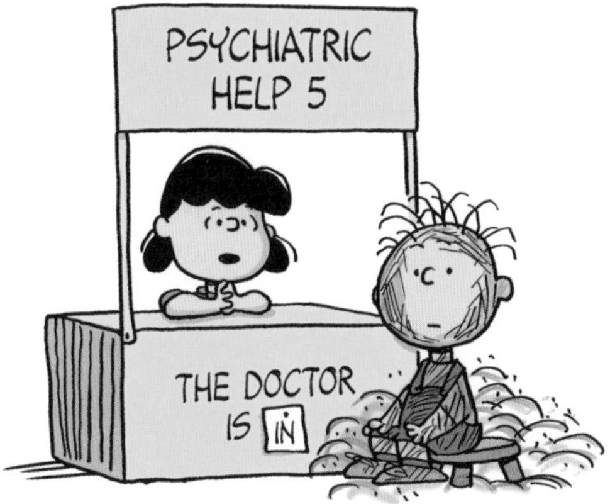
PSYCHIATRIC
HELP 5
THE DOCTOR
IS IN

"I don't know, Pigpen. When I look at you, all I see is dirt and dust. You don't need a psychiatrist. . . . You need an archaeologist!"

—*Lucy*

Be
ALERT

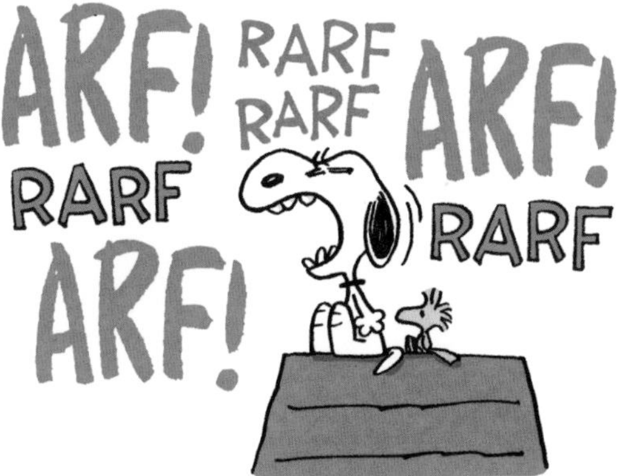
ARF!
RARF
RARF
ARF!
RARF
RARF
ARF!

Be

PASSIONATE

"Nobody told me life was going to be this hard!"
—*Sally*

Be
SUPER

Be
THOUGHTFUL

Be
TOUGH

"Those kids over at the playground think they're so tough. Well, I'm not out to start any trouble, but I'm also not afraid of them! I'm taking the advice of Theodore Roosevelt: Speak softly and carry a big beagle!"
  —Sally

Be

Happy

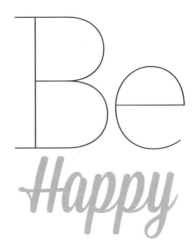

"There really is nothing more attractive than a nice smile. . . . Within bounds of reason, of course."
—*Charlie Brown*

Be
INVOLVED

Be
PROFESSIONAL

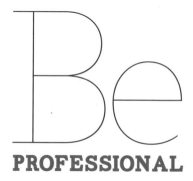

"How did you get started as a barber? Is there room for advancement? What about health care? Is it a good career for women?"
   —*Peppermint Patty*

Be
GIVING

"Here Charlie Brown, I've got a piece of candy for you. I'll brush off the lint and scrape this old gum off the best I can."
    —*Pig-Pen*

Be
OUTSTANDING

Be
Impressive

Be
PERCEPTIVE

Linus: Doesn't looking at all these stars make you feel sort of insignificant, Charlie Brown?
Charlie Brown: No . . . I'm so insignificant already it doesn't bother me!

Be

ATTENTIVE

Linus: What are you drawing?
Sally: The sun. Don't look at it too closely. You'll hurt your eyes!

Be
Free

Be
COURAGEOUS

Be
PREPARED

"Yes, Ma'am . . . it's cold outside. I'd like an ice cream cone, please."
    —*Charlie Brown*

Be

DARING

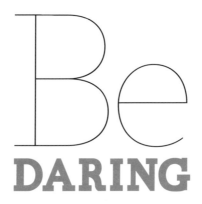

"It takes courage to sail in uncharted waters."
   —*Snoopy*

BELIEVE!